Just Where Does God Live?

By Scott J. Brown
Illustrated by Enedina Vasquez

WinePress WP Publishing Kids

WinePress Publishing (PO Box 428, Enumclaw, WA 98022) functions only as book publisher. As such, the ultimate design, content, editorial accuracy, and views expressed or implied in this work are those of the author.

ISBN 13: 978-1-60615-016-0
ISBN 10: 1-60615-016-2
Library of Congress Catalog Card Number: 209928813

Printed in South Korea.

To Parker and Christopher Brown and to Nate Newman.
May you never forget that with God in your heart, all things are possible.

*You are
God's dream
come true!*

Scott Brown

In a small town down south
Lived two six-year-old boys
Who loved baseball and tennis
And playing with toys.

They also loved learning
And thought school was great.

They were the best of friends

Named Parker and Nate.

They talked about things
They wanted to know,
Like how snakes can slither
And where the clouds go.

They wondered 'bout dinosaurs
And where they all went,
And when mommies say "maybe"
What that actually meant.

But there was one question
They talked much about,
For as much as they tried,
They couldn't figure it out.

So they set out to find
If someone could give
The answer to the question,

They ran to their neighbor,
A third grader named Kevin,
Who said right away,
"Of course God lives in heaven."

"If God lives in heaven,"
Parker wondered out loud,
"Then how can God see me
Through the big puffy cloud?"

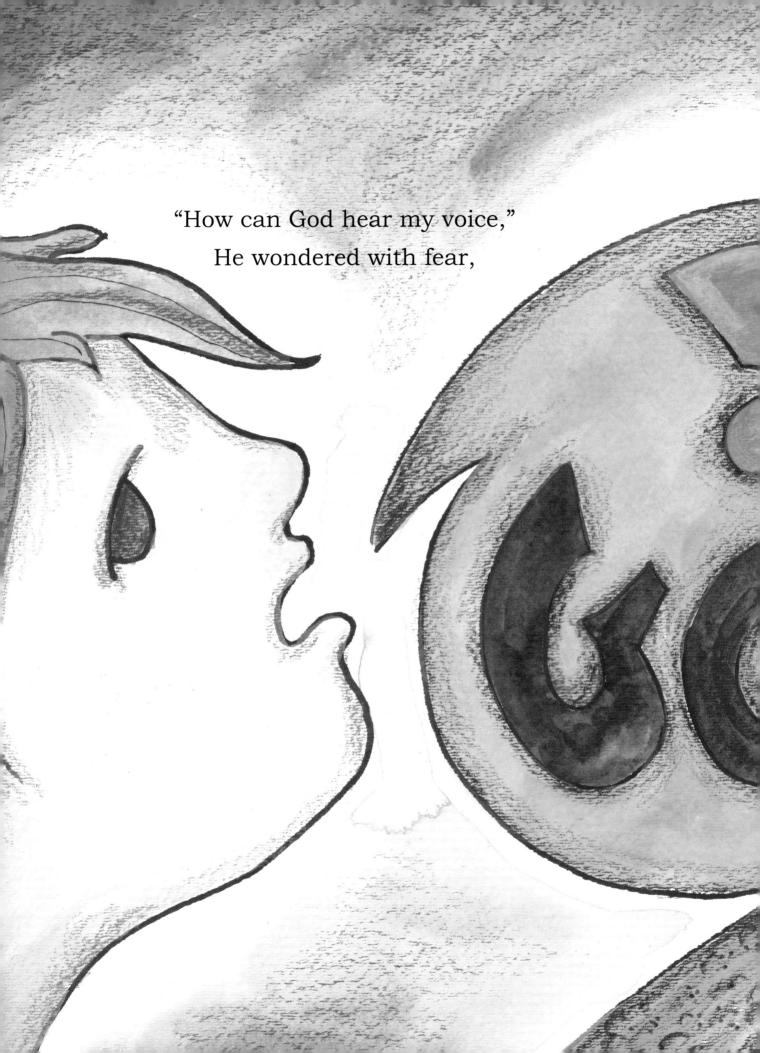

"How can God hear my voice,"
He wondered with fear,

"If God's way up there
And I'm way down here?"

So on the boys went
In search of the truth,
When they found an old fisherman
Who was missing a tooth.

"Please sir, help us!
We have to find out.
Just where does God live?
Do you have any doubt?"

The man told the boys
As he reeled in his perch,

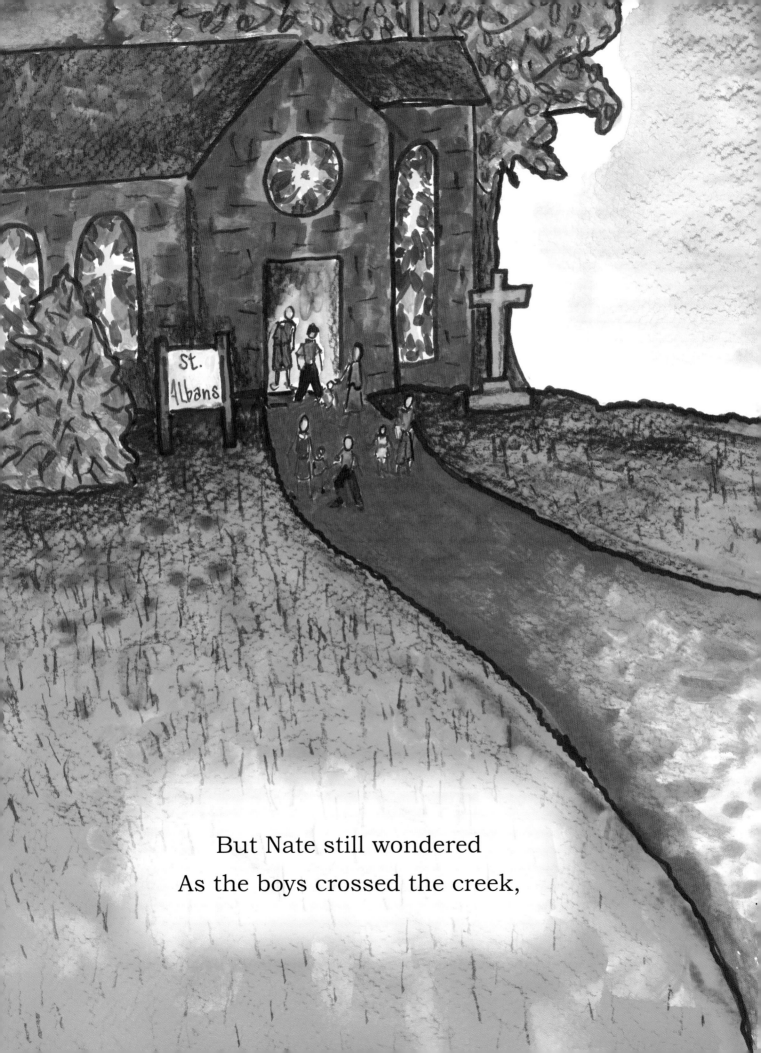

But Nate still wondered
As the boys crossed the creek,

How could God live somewhere
You see once a week?

As the boys headed home
They were happy to see,
A smart girl named Bella
Dressing dolls by a tree.

"Excuse me," said Parker,
"Could you put down that comb,
And tell us if you know
Just where God calls home?"

Bella said, "You boys are silly.
You're just such a hassle.

Any girl can tell you,
God lives in a pink castle."

That answer was good,
And it made the boys think.

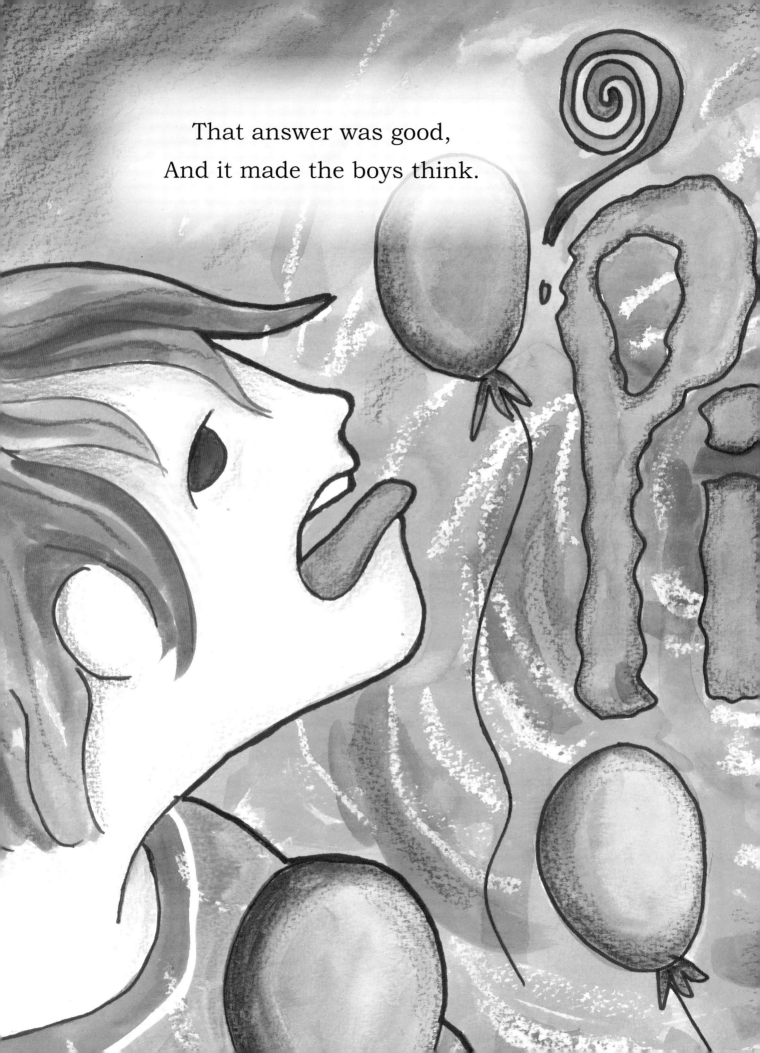

Yet inside they wondered,
Would God really choose pink?

So the boys made a deal
And agreed with great force,
That tonight their question
Would go straight to the source.

As the boys lay in bed
In their houses that night,
Their moms tucked them in,
Their dads turned out the light.

And with all that they had
And all they could give,

They both said to God,
"Just where do you live?"

The answer came back
Just as clear as a bell.
It was God's voice;
They somehow could tell.

God said, "I do live in heaven,
I'll wait for you here.
I'm also in church
Every day of the year.

You see my dear sons,
I live in all spaces.
I live in all people,
I live in all places.

With great love and care,
I create the world's parts.
But my favorite place,
Is inside of your hearts."

In the morning they woke,
And they knew they must tell,
The wonderful news
They now both knew so well.

With God in their hearts,
They couldn't wait to share,

Once you've found God in one place,

You can find God everywhere.

Where do you

think God lives?

Draw some pictures of

where you think God lives!

Who are you going to tell

about the places God lives?